THE GOLDEN RAFT

Also by Dennis Michael Dutton

Stepson

The Golden Raft Comes Home

After the Golden Raft

What the Heck Have You Done Now, Kate?

The Rose of Majorca

Coming soon

H E R M A N

THE GOLDEN RAFT

By

Dennis Michael Dutton

Published by Dennis Michael Dutton

Copyright © 2014 Dennis Michael Dutton

All rights reserved

In accordance with the U.S. Copyright Act of 1975, the reproducing, scanning, uploading, and electronic sharing of any part of this book without permission of the publisher is unlawful piracy and the theft of the author's intellectual property. If you would like to use material from the book (other than for review purposes), prior written permission must be obtained from the publisher. Thank you for supporting the author's rights.

The characters and events in this book are fictitious. Any similarity to real persons, living or dead, is coincidental and not intended by the author.

Cover design by Dennis Michael Dutton

ISBN-13: 978-1500708856

ISBN-10: 1500708852

Prologue

"$150,000! Do you believe that? One hundred and fifty thousand dollars for a three bedroom and two bathrooms home, and it doesn't even have a swimming pool?"

The real estate woman looked startled when I raised my voice. *Well, you can look startled and be hanged*, I thought. *Where I came from, $150,000 would be enough to purchase a mansion, and she has the nerve to say, "the price isn't too bad, considering the neighborhood."*

"As long as we're talking about the neighborhood, how about finding us a house with three bedrooms, two baths, a screened-in porch and a medium-sized pool in the neighborhood of thirty thousand dollars? Now that's the kind of neighbors I want." From the expression on her face, she wasn't even going to answer that one, and from the look that Gail, my wife, was giving me, the only choice that I had in the matter was the option to pay cash or to finance it.

I chose to pay a hundred thousand dollars down, and finance the balance for twenty years. This would leave us enough cash to purchase the swimming pool and the screened-in porch plus any other changes that we might want to make. Oh well, it could be worse, we could be shoveling snow in western New York state instead of enjoying the sunshine here in central Florida. I guess it isn't going to be too bad after all. The house is on a corner lot and the present owners have worked hard to do a good job with the landscaping.

The lawn is St. Augustine grass and there are two citrus trees, one is Temple orange and the other is a Navel. In addition, there are three palm trees, four pines and a Live Oak. Also, there are shrubs and other green, red, and yellow plants surrounding the house.

Before signing the purchase offer, we took another tour of the house and yard. I even went up into the attic to check it out. *Maybe, just maybe, we'll be lucky and find some antiques in the attic that will be valuable enough to offset the high price of the house* I thought as I crawled around shining the flashlight into all the corners. Unfortunately, I didn't find a thing, not one darn thing of value anyway, but it did give the real estate lady time to write up the purchase offer.

Gail and I both signed the purchase offer and gave the realtor a check for the deposit and started back to our motel to wait for her to call and let us know if it was going to be accepted or not by the sellers. We stopped at a fast-food restaurant for lunch before returning to the motel.

When we arrived at our room, the phone was ringing. I unlocked the door and Gail grabbed the phone and said, "Hello." For the next five minutes, she was only able to utter a few uh-huhs because the real estate woman was talking fast and furious. Finally, the lady ran out of wind and Gail said that "Friday would be all right with us," and hung up the phone.

"Friday would be all right for what," I wanted to know.

"Calm down, calm down, all she said was that the sellers accepted our offer and the closing will be Friday morning."

"Whoopee! Whoopee-snoopee," I said, "$398.98 a month until the year 2029, and that's after making a one-hundred-thousand dollar down payment. Why, they should be jumping up and down with joy. The down payment is twice what the place is worth, and the rest is all profit. I'll bet she's been trying to reach us since five minutes after we left her. It shouldn't have taken very long to tell the owners that she had a couple of New York suckers on the string to the tune of a hundred and fifty thousand bucks."

Boy, they sure work fast with real estate closings in this state. Four days from purchase offer to closing. Why, in New York State, the average time from offer to closing was six weeks and then only if there weren't any problems. The main reason is that Florida uses Title Insurance instead of Warranty Deeds to transfer property and that is a lot quicker. The problem is that the seller has to be ready to move when they accept an offer. The couple that we purchased our house from had already bought a mobile home in an adult park, and they were in the process of moving when we came to look at the house, and they assured us that they would be all moved out.

Anyway, on Friday we signed the papers, paid our money, and drove to our new home with key in hand. This was the largest expenditure that we had ever made and, by golly, we planned to enjoy every minute of it. When we arrived at our new home, we found that the sellers weren't completely moved out yet and hadn't made any attempt to clean the way they had promised. In fact, we had to make three trips with our van just to get them all moved out.

Gail is a softy, especially when it comes to elderly people, so when the lady told her how tired she was after such a long and busy day, Gail offered to do the cleaning for her. So, I spent the first night in our new home with a broom in my hand. I guess it wasn't so bad after all, because they were a nice couple and they really appreciated the help.

I should have known that Gail was going to clean the whole place anyway, no matter how clean it was when we got there. This gave her a chance to check all of the nooks and crannies for "livestock" (cockroaches and spiders) before we moved in and put roach powder wherever she had to. Fortunately, they had been meticulous in their roach prevention program so, by continuing along the same way they did, we would keep them under control.

We started moving into the house on Saturday morning with the first vanload from the storage building arriving at seven a.m. and by the time noon rolled around, the storage building was empty and everything that we had brought with us was in and ready to use. At about one o'clock, the truck from Sears arrived with the new refrigerator and microwave oven and then we were ready to get settled.

The next couple of weeks were spent arranging things the way we wanted them to be and making small purchases to brighten up the place. Sunday afternoon we took a trip to Orlando to one of the plazas to see a display of swimming pools to try to get an idea about the size of pool that we were going to be able to afford. Before the afternoon was over, we had purchased an in-ground pool with all of the extras for a measly thirty thousand dollars.

Man oh man, if those salesmen were chicken pluckers, there wouldn't be a chicken left in the state with a feather on it. Anyway, the contract called for them to install a twenty by forty foot pool, complete with filter, ladder, steps, and diving board. In addition to that, there was a screen house over it to keep it clean and the bugs out. All of this to be done in twenty-one days without fail. The only thing that was left out was what would happen if they didn't live up to the contract. I guess that wasn't going to be a problem anyway, because at ten o'clock on Monday morning, a truck arrived with the backhoe ready to dig the hole. A few minutes later, the boss showed up with the plans and a building permit from the city, and they were ready to go to work.

While the boss was looking for a place to dump the dirt from the hole, the other two men staked it out and began digging. The first and second truckloads went along pretty well but, when they started to dig the third one, the backhoe hooked into a cypress tree stump that was buried in one corner and they had to tear it apart to get it out because it was too large to move in one piece. The backhoe wasn't strong enough to lift it anyway, so he just kept ripping and pulling until it broke into pieces that could be lifted.

As they were lifting one large section up and trying to get it on the truck, the piece fell and, when it hit the ground, a rectangular shaped wooden box that had been caught in the roots was jarred loose and fell right in front of Gail and me. I reached down and picked it up to throw on the truck, when Gail said, "Wait a minute before you throw that away; it looks like an antique." Well, if you want to get my attention fast, just say the magic word, and that's *antique*.

I knocked the sand off the box and rubbed it on my pant leg to see if it would clean up enough so that I could get some idea about what it was. At first, it appeared to be just a heavy block of wood about six inches by six inches and twelve inches long. As I continued to rub it on my pant leg, I discovered what looked like a pair of brass-colored hinges. "Well I'll be darned; maybe it's a box of some kind." I gave it to Gail and she took it into the kitchen, rinsed it off in the sink, and dried it with a rough towel. When all of the dirt was removed, it revealed a complex design that covered the entire outside of the box.

Gail and I both tried to open it without any success but, because of the design, we decided that it may have some value, so she wrapped the box in the towel and laid it in the cupboard under the sink, and we went back out to where the men were digging the hole for the pool.

When the truck was loaded and driven away, the backhoe operator asked if we really found a box, or if it was just a piece of wood. "To tell you the truth, we don't know what it is. When Gail cleaned it up, it still looked like a box, but we haven't found out how to open it yet." His interest in the box might have lasted longer except that the boss came back, they began checking measurements in the hole against the ones on the plan, and we drifted away from the side yard and into the kitchen again. After the door was closed, Gail retrieved the box from under the sink and took it to my shop.

For the next two hours, we did everything we could think of to get that darn box to open up. We shook it, banged it, and even dropped it on the floor once, by accident, and it still wouldn't budge. The more we tried to get it open, the less we seemed to be accomplishing. If the box was a box at all, then there had to be a way to open it. But on the other hand, if it wasn't a box after all, but just a piece of wood, then whoever it was that took the time to do the fancy artwork and go to the bother of attaching the hinges, must have been a real practical joker.

Later that night after our two daughters, Rebecca and Jackie, had gone to bed, Gail and I retreated to my shop again to start another round at trying to open the box. This time we decided to be "scientific," in the approach, which means that Gail would allow me to use a small hammer. Actually, I did use a small hammer to tap the ends and sides in an effort to find if it was solid or hollow, but the results of my tapping were inconclusive.

It seemed as though everything we did pointed us in the direction of the box not actually being a box, but a well-decorated piece of wood with a pair of hinges. I polished the hinges with a rouge cloth and was surprised at the amount of luster that appeared. "What if they aren't brass after all, and are made of gold instead," I asked. That would really make us more inquisitive than we were now, if that was possible.

"There are so many things to wonder about, it's beginning to feel like a good mystery story," Gail said.

Shortly after midnight, when it began to look as though we were not making any headway in our efforts to get the box open, we decided to use the box like a printers block and, by putting ink on it, make a print of the design on the outside. I didn't have any printer's ink, so I took the inkpad that came with the rubber stamp and patted it all over one side. Gail took the box and pressed it down on a clean sheet of white paper and, sure enough, we had a print. There didn't appear to be a left or right or, for that matter, a top or bottom either, so we assigned the box a top, and from there we were able to make a complete print of it. On the bottom, there appeared to be a map of some sort but, since we couldn't identify it, we tended to ignore it. When the prints were finished and the box re-cleaned, I put the prints on the desk and we shifted them around trying to find the proper sequence, but the order apparently didn't make any difference, so we left them and went to bed.

For the next couple of days there was so much activity in the yard with the contractors building the pool that we just left the box in my shop and thought about it when we had a chance. The extra time gave both of us an opportunity to gather our individual thoughts and ideas so, when the other activities slowed down a little, we were ready again to try our luck with the box. Mostly, we just sat and looked at it and talked, and in the end arrived at a consensus of opinion. First of all, the box was a box. Second, the design on the outside appeared to be Indian, so a copy of the print should be taken to the museum to see if they were able to identify it. And third, we would continue trying to get it open.

Another three days passed before we had an opportunity to take the print to the museum in Orlando and ask them to compare it with artifacts from known Indian tribes from this area. The curator of the museum was extremely interested in the design but was unable to match it with anything from local Indians.

The closest that he could come was from the tribes from the mountains of Peru and Columbia. In addition to that, it was sixteenth century. The curator checked several reference books, called two local experts on Peruvian Indians, and found that very few relics survived the Spanish conquistadors. Whatever there was from that period was being closely held by the Government of Peru and was on public display, but remained the property of Peru.

"Where did you obtain these prints?" he asked. "Were they left to you, or did you purchase them? They're beautiful."

We looked at one another before answering and then Gail said, "We made them from a box that we found in our backyard."

"Where is it? Where's the box right now? Do you still have it in your possession?"

"Well, yes, we still have it, but it's at home. Why do you want it?"

"Don't you people know that the state owns all Indian artifacts and that it's my job and responsibility to make a complete investigation of all archeological sites?" He seemed to be getting a little excited about his authority and more so about our ignorance, so I attempted to calm him down a bit.

"Look pal, we're not here for a lecture about the laws of the state. All we want to know is where the box came from."

The curator leaned forward in his chair, picked up a pen from his desk, and said, "Would you please tell me your name and address?"

It was clear that he was going to be all business from now on, so I mustered up my very best smile and asked, "Why?"

"What do you mean 'why'?" he practically yelled, "So I can have the area investigated as a possible archeological site, that's why."

"No, no, no, you're not going to hold up the construction of our swimming pool so that a bunch of weirdo's can make mud pies in our back yard all summer, uh-uh." As I was answering him, Gail and I backed away and eased toward the door.

"Do you understand your responsibility as a resident of this state with regard to archeological sites?" he asked.

I could see that he wasn't going to give up without a fight so, as we reached the door and started out, I said, "We're sorry to have bothered you and thank you for the information, good bye."

When we reached the street, I suggested that we leave the van in the parking lot for the time being and mix with the afternoon crowd on the sidewalk so that we could not be followed. Gail and I drifted along with the shoppers.

After an hour of window shopping, we walked back to the parking lot and got our van. Driving north on Orange Blossom Trail at this hour of the day was pretty wild to say the least. It looked as though everybody in Orlando was leaving at the same time, and we were in the middle of it.

When we reached home, Gail went to the kitchen to get supper started while I secured our papers in my shop.

For the next couple of days we enjoyed our pool and just being at home.

Chapter 1

In the year 1532, the Spanish soldier and adventurer, Francisco Pizarro, landed in Peru with a small force of men. By guile and by the use of firearms, Pizarro made the Inca Empire a Spanish possession. In 1535, on the banks of the Rimac River, Pizarro founded the Peruvian capital city of Ciudad de los Reyes (City of the Kings). It is the present day site of the capital of Peru, Lima. Pizarro's troops spread out in small groups, looted, and plundered the Inca Indian villages. Thousands of Indians were maimed and murdered and the villages were burned by the marauding soldiers.

***

Ugma and Meta had been united as one for less than a year when the soldiers stormed their village in search of gold and silver. Fortunately, most of the villagers were either working in the mines or tending the children about a mile away when they arrived. The few that were there hid in the forest until the soldiers left.

"These murderers must be stopped, Ugma," Meta said. "They're killing so many of our people that soon we shall also die." Tears ran down her cheeks as she tried to sort through the piles of rubble strewn both inside and outside their hut. The piles were all that was left of their personal possessions now that the raid was over and the soldiers had gone. Everything of value was either missing or broken and discarded. Their village was a shambles. Others were not as fortunate as they were; their huts were burned and in some cases, even the livestock was killed.

"Even if I did know how to stop them, there isn't anyone that would listen to me; I've only been an elder for a short time."

For nearly three years, stories had passed from village to village about the strange soldiers and their insane quest for silver and gold. The elders and even the great council had spent many hours trying to formulate a plan of defense but, so far, the only thing that worked was to hide while the soldiers took whatever they wanted. "They have so many men to fight us that we don't have a chance, and soon they will find the main gold and silver supply and kill us anyway," Ugma answered.

"Please, Ugma," she cried, "You must think of a way to save us."

This, of course, was easier said than done because all of the chiefs in the country had been trying to find a way to rid their land of these strangers and had failed. *Besides, who am I to think that I could save even myself, let alone the whole country?* "Meta, I can't do it, you know very well that I'm a wood carver, not a warrior."

Until recently, all that Ugma had ever done was to study woodcarving as an apprentice. Now, of course, he was a full-fledged wood carver and had joined the ranks of the elders of the village. In fact, he was the youngest elder and nobody was interested in listening to what he had to say.

For the next few days, Ugma kept as busy as possible in an effort to avoid Meta's tearful pleadings. Staying out of sight was not too difficult when you were a wood carver, because there was always the excuse that, "I spent all day in the woods searching for trees to cut down."

Early in the evening, as Ugma was preparing to return home from the wooded hillside south of the village, he noticed some movement at the far end of the valley. Several minutes passed as Ugma jockeyed for a better position from which he could observe the disturbance. "Oh no, it's the soldiers again!"

Dropping his pack and ax, he started running as fast as he could to the village.

"Quick, Meta, we have to get everyone out of the village. The killers are on the way here right now; I saw them hiding in the valley."

They ran from hut to hut quietly alerting the villagers to leave as soon as they could and not to worry about their possessions because if they didn't hurry, they would be murdered. "Leave the livestock, especially the dogs, so they will have something to steal, otherwise they'll come looking for us."

Ugma stood by the last hut waiting for the few stragglers to pass by on their way to the protection of the woods. "Stay here, Meta. I'm going to make a final check of the huts," Ugma whispered but, before he could get to even the closest one, the dogs started barking on the other side of the village, and he knew that the soldiers had arrived. They ducked down as low as they could and ran to the nearest trees and on into the dense underbrush. From there, they went to the stream, waded to the middle, and walked as quickly and quietly as they could for a couple hundred feet before leaving the water. This was necessary so that the dogs could not pick up their scent and track them to the hiding place.

In the distance, Ugma could hear the snarling and yelping of the dogs and the shouting of the men as they wielded their swords and clubs to protect themselves. The villagers ran faster now and tried not to listen as the snarls turned to wails as the Spanish slaughtered the dogs.

After about ten minutes of running, the villagers fell to the ground exhausted. Through the puffing, Meta's tears began again, "When will they leave us alone?" she sobbed. "I haven't even finished cleaning up the mess from the last raid. This time they'll probably burn our hut too."

Swinging around into a sitting position, Ugma cradled Meta's head in his lap and wiped away the tears. "Oh, God, please help us," he pleaded, looking up at the sky and rocking back and forth in unison with her sobbing." It was beginning to look as though not all of the Gods together would be strong enough to protect them from the soldiers.

Their village consisted of fifty-nine people: seven elderly, thirty of working and childbearing age, and twenty-two children. Because of the gold and silver mines that they owned collectively, they were able to purchase all of their food stocks and hire hunters from the other villages for their meat supply. By doing this, they could concentrate all of their efforts on the operation of the mines.

Most of the gold and silver was shipped in wooden boxes and, because it was so valuable, the boxes had to be pretty fancy. Ugma's job was to build ornate boxes. Each box was of a different design and carved with scenes such as birds, or people, or dogs, or llamas, or sometimes a combination of many things. The important thing was to be original, because the buyers sometimes sold the boxes separately to earn extra money for themselves.

All of the elderly in their village still worked at the mines and thirteen of the older children were working as apprentices. Although there were not very many of them, they accomplished quite a bit by working together, and they still had time for playing, praying, and raising their families. The women also worked at the mines except while they were having babies, and then they helped take care of all of the younger ones. Meta did not have any children yet, so she worked at the mine during the daytime, and took care of their hut at night.

Also at night, she helped the other women of the village with community projects such as blanket and quilt making. These jobs required more than one person, so the women and children got together at night and worked as a group.

While Meta and the other women worked on the community projects, the men spent their leisure time working on specialty items that they were able to sell for private profit. This was the only way a person could better themselves financially within the village. Several evenings a week, Ugma worked building wooden boxes and decorating them. Boxes that were not purchased by other members of the village, he saved for the gold traders. Sometimes, late at night, Meta helped with the boxes. Ugma taught her how to smooth and polish them, and she enjoyed doing what was considered *men's work*. It also gave them more hours in the day that they could spend together.

Chapter 2

Ugma arrived at his home village a short time before noon and went to the hut of the senior elder at once to report what he had seen. Arto, the senior elder, welcomed Ugma into his hut and asked him about the trip. After Ugma finished telling Arto the fate of their friends, he said, "We must call a meeting of the elders at once and make plans to be out of the village before dark."

"Slow down a little," Arto said. "What you are proposing will affect every member of our village and they need time to discuss this plan and decide for themselves."

Arto had only been the senior elder for a short time, and he wondered if the other elders would be upset with him for calling a meeting in the middle of the day. Ugma assured him that this might be their last day if they didn't get moving, so never mind what the others thought and call the meeting for right now. Ugma went to the two mines to get everyone back to the village while Arto got all the other people together.

In less than an hour, all the villagers were assembled for the meeting and Arto started by saying a prayer to all the Gods and asking for guidance. Then he turned to Ugma and said, "Ugma has just returned from the two villages by the river, and he has asked for this meeting to tell you what he found. After he is finished, we will decide what we're going to do about it."

"Last night I was sent by Arto to the other villages to see if the soldiers were still stealing their gold, silver, and animals. In the first village, everyone was dead. Yes, everyone was dead. They had been dead for several days. Before I left, I counted them to make sure that no one was hiding that we could bring here to live with us. However, they were all dead. In the next village, it was the same. They were all dead too! All of our friends in those two villages are dead, and now we must prepare to leave this, our home. Today we have to leave forever or we too will be dead, just like our friends."

Ugma stretched his arms upwards and began to pray. "O God, we stand before you today asking you to preserve our lives. Guide us in everything we do or say. Show us your plan for our lives. Give me a plan that will keep us safe and lead us to another land where we can live and give praise to you. Please God, show me your plan."

Ugma slowly lowered his arms and began to speak as though in a trance. "All of the raids by the soldiers have been from the south, so we will go north. We will go north to the great river and then follow the river to the sea. We will travel for many weeks to reach the sea. Some of us may die along the way, but if we don't go, all of us will die right here in our huts! There is no choice, north to the great river and east with the river to the sea is the only way we can go, and we have to go now, today, before dark.

"The plan is simple. We will take as much food and clothing and gold and silver as we can safely carry, and all the rest we must leave behind. We will start each morning before the sun comes up, walk for four hours, then rest for two hours, and then walk for another four hours. After two more hours of rest, we will continue until the sun goes down.

"This pace will be maintained until we reach the river Ucayali. At that time, we will try to buy or barter for some rafts or boats from the River People. If the River People refuse to sell us what we need, then we will cut trees and build our own. The most important thought for all of us as we decide on the articles to take and the ones to leave behind, is this: will it help me to provide for my family, or can I wear it to keep warm and dry.

"All men are to take only the tools necessary for their trade; women will take only clothes and cooking utensils. Everything else must be left here. Of course, we will also need to carry the gold and silver necessary for our future needs. Remember, this will be a very long trip so do not pack anything that you cannot carry easily. Hurry now and prepare to leave. We must leave soon, before the soldiers come to kill us. Hurry! Hurry! Everyone has to get ready to leave."

As the villagers hurried about packing their possessions and preparing to leave, Ugma and Meta sat in their hut and prayed to the Gods for special guidance on their journey. Meta was the only one of the women that knew for sure that they would never see this village again, and she tried to keep from crying or showing any emotion in an effort to let Ugma know that she knew he was doing the right thing.

The big problem for Ugma was that their people had lived in this same village for more than three hundred years, and now he was asking them all to pack their belongings and move away forever. "Please, God of the Future," he prayed, "make this decision the right one. Don't let us leave our village without our having to." Meta stood by the doorway of the hut and watched as the others scurried about preparing to leave. If only they knew, perhaps they would make different choices about what to take and what to leave behind. They all seemed to be packing as though they would be home again tomorrow; this of course was not true. They would never see their homes again.

Ugma, Arto, and the other elders assembled in the center of the village and helped everyone get ready to start the long march to a new home, perhaps even a new land. Arto counted to see that everyone was there and ready. "My fellow villagers and my family ... this is a day we shall never forget ... even our children and their children will remember that we were forced to leave our homes and our loved ones that have died before us ... so that we may live in peace." He paused for a moment and then said, "Ugma has been visited by the Gods and he alone has been shown the way. Because of this, Ugma will be our leader for as long as we are searching for our new home. I will still be the senior elder, but Ugma is responsible for our safe journey."

Ugma stepped forward and said loudly, "At the head of the line I want three strong men to lead and protect the rest of us from danger. Next, will come the women and small children, one child for each woman. After that, I want the elderly with an older child that shall assist them and stay with them throughout the journey. Our main concern here is to pair everyone in a helping position with someone who may need some assistance. Don't worry about who your partner is today, because you can all change tomorrow if you want to."

"It's time to leave, is everyone ready?"

Without waiting for an answer, Ugma and Meta went to the end of the line and slowly walked to the front checking packs and halters on the llamas and talking to each person as they moved forward. Everything looked to be in order and it was time for them to say goodbye to their homes.

Chapter 3

With a wave of his hat, Ugma signaled the men at the front of the line to begin the first part of the journey that would take them to the Ucayali River. The river was about one hundred miles away and, for the first few days, they would be able to travel fifteen to twenty miles a day. As they got closer to the river, the jungle would become denser and, on some days, it would be difficult to go even two or three miles.

It was easy going now. Most of them were enjoying the change from their usual work schedule, and the conversation between them had a happy note to it. *Keep smiling*, Ugma thought, *the farther and farther we go, the less you're going to have to smile about. I only hope and pray that I will be able to live up to Arto's expectations and lead us safely to a new home. Actually, I never did say that I had received special guidance or, for that matter, we never even discussed a plan. It's beginning to look as though Arto had the idea that our move was necessary, and if someone else wanted to volunteer to take the responsibility for the move then he would let them. Well, here I am,* Ugma thought, *the volunteer leader of my own villagers and I do not have any idea where we are going. More importantly, is that we are not sitting around in our huts waiting for the soldiers to kill us. We are quickly moving away from the danger.*

Their best route would be to follow the Great River east as far as it went and then maybe they would find a place for their new home. When they reached the river, Ugma hoped they could trade their llamas for the rafts and boats they needed to continue their journey. If not, they would have to buy them and then try to sell or give away the llamas. Either way, it was still going to be all right because they were alive, and that was the most important thing.

As soon as the sun dropped below the tops of the trees, Ugma called the front men and told them to stop for the night. "Everybody fix something to eat for tonight and enough for tomorrow morning too, so that we can get an early start."

Most of the villagers were restless and it was quite difficult for them to get any sleep. *Sleep well my village family*, Ugma thought. *In a few days we will be at the river and, by then, this whole trip will be real enough to you.* The days that followed kept everyone so busy and tired no one questioned where, how far, or how long the trip would last.

If we have any luck at all, we should reach the river tomorrow afternoon and have the rafts loaded before dark, Ugma thought. *When the first light of the new day comes over the trees, we will start down the river.* Men and women worked together unloading the llamas and setting up camp for the night. It was not very long before everyone was settled down and Ugma had time to think about the next few days, where they were going and, more importantly, when they would stop and build a new village.

The night went by quickly, and now it was time to load everything and start again for the river. Questions kept popping into Ugma's mind. *How many rafts are we going to need? How many rafts are we going to be able to get? What should we take, and what will we have to leave behind? How many llamas will we be able to take on the rafts along with enough feed for them? I sure hope that I can remember everything. One thing is sure, by the time the sun goes down tonight all of these questions will have been answered and another group will be asked. However, I will be ready for them with the right answers; of that much I'm positive.* "On to the river," he shouted and the journey started again.

Fortunately, the good spirits among the villagers continued today as they had been yesterday and the miles were covered very swiftly. In just a few minutes, they would arrive at the village and the bartering for the rafts would begin.

"When we get to the village," Arto shouted, "I want all of you to stay with your belongings except the elders. They will help me purchase the rafts."

For the most part, everyone waited patiently as Arto, Ugma, and the other elders went ahead to the river village to arrange for the rafts. As they approached the village, two guards came to meet them to find out what they were after. Arto had visited this village in the past, and they knew that he was not there for a fight, so he was invited in to explain why they were there. He talked to the elders for a while about the strangers and how they had destroyed so many villages and killed the people in them, and why they had decided to leave and find another home. When this was over, he asked about purchasing the rafts and also hiring some men to teach them how to sail them. Because they had never been on a raft, it was difficult to know how many they would need and how large the rafts should be. Maybe, if they did not act dumb, the river people wouldn't try to cheat them.

Soon it was decided that they would purchase three large Balsa rafts, each one large enough to carry about thirty-five people and their belongings. The extra space would be used to carry the llamas and the food for them. The rafts were made from balsa wood as the name implied, and were very light in weight, this they hoped would make it easier to handle them and allow the villagers to go faster on the river.

After a hurried meeting of the elders, Arto traded all the adults and some of the young llamas for the rafts, leaving them with just five females and three males to take on the journey. By doing that, they would be able to have enough for breeding and it would take a lot less food. A very good idea by Arto, the less food they needed for the llamas, the more food they could take for themselves. Yes, Arto was a very smart leader.

The loading of the rafts was a happy time for all of them, mostly because they had never been on a raft before and it was a new experience. Three men were assigned to each raft and they would teach the villagers how to operate it. All men, women, and all children over the age of ten years would learn how to operate it; those were Arto's orders.

The rafts were thirty feet long and about fifteen feet wide. In the center section was a raised bench area called a pumacuri. The pumacuri had a yarin or canopy over it to protect the people from the sun and the rain. Cooking facilities were available on a tripod at the stern of the raft that was covered with dirt so that you could build a fire in the dirt and not endanger anything else with the fire. Overall, they were going to be quite comfortable and it appeared that everyone was looking forward to the voyage.

The voyage to where, that was a question to be reconciled with soon enough but, for the moment, there were more pressing things to occupy Ugma's mind, such as learning how to operate the raft. It would not look very good, if all the ten-year-olds knew how to sail and he didn't, so he turned his thoughts to becoming a sailor.

"What happens if you fall into the water?" Ugma asked.

"You swim to the raft or to the shore, the instructor laughed," and then said, "you know, swim with your hands and feet, like this" and he jumped into the water and showed the villagers what he meant by swimming. They must have looked pretty dumb to him when he got out of the water, because he told them that there wouldn't be any more sailing lessons until everyone knew how to swim. Everyone, he said, would have to know how or else they couldn't get on his raft and that was final.

They all took swimming lessons for the next four days, until they could swim well enough to pass his inspection. Ugma could swim about one hundred feet, and he made a mental note to never get any farther away from the shore or the raft then that.

The men teaching the villagers told them that their biggest worry when swimming was the piranha fish. They suggested that whenever the villagers wanted to go in the water that first they should throw in a piece of meat to see if there were any around. If any piranha fish were there, they would eat the meat so fast that their jumping around would really stir up the water and no one would need to wonder what kind of fish they were; they would know right away. Swimming rule number one: if you throw in a piece of meat and you can see the piranha fish eating it, stay away from the water.

Now that all the villagers could swim, it was time to get back to learning how to sail a raft or rather to steer a raft, and so the lessons started again. This time everyone was more confident of themselves and, therefore, could learn faster. Almost everyone had been able to get rid of his or her fear of water; learning to swim was a good idea even if they were not going on the rafts. Once again, the Gods were looking out for them.

Chapter 4

Because the villagers didn't have any huts to live in, they all stayed on the rafts and made them their home. It was good that they had because, when the time came to leave, all that was necessary was to load the llamas and drift on down the river.

"We leave in the morning," Arto said, and now they knew that their life on the water was about to start.

It would be a good life, Ugma thought, *a very good life. The rafts will be our homes until we find a new place for the village, and a new way to support ourselves.* The chances of finding a gold or silver mine were probably not too good either. Today was not the day to worry about that. Today, Meta and Ugma would spend together planning their future and remembering their past.

It wouldn't be necessary for Arto to give the order to load the rafts, because everyone and everything was ready to go long before daylight.

They were all anxious to leave. The sky looked as though it was going to be a nice day, so they might just as well get started. "Time to go," Ugma shouted. "Push the rafts out into the current and let's get moving!" The crew of each raft took its turn poling their way out into the river current and steering with the river as they had been taught. For the moment, everything was going fine. They had no way of knowing that if they went twenty-five miles a day, it would still take them more than three months to reach the ocean. In fact, they didn't even know what the ocean was.

However, when the time came, the villagers would learn. They would learn because that's the kind of people they were. Ten days ago none of them had ever seen the river, but now they were able to swim, catch fish, and steer the rafts. All of these things were new to them, and they learned how to do them. Maybe the reason they were able to learn so fast was because all of them had a trade that they had learned, so concentrating on the subject being taught was easy. Not all villagers have had training the way they had. Their elders believed that all of them needed to be trained for a job that would contribute to the group as a whole. When the time came to learn about new things, they would learn. And that's how it was.

Day one on the river was uneventful, a quick rain shower, and then the hot sun all day long. It was good to have the river breeze to help cool it down and the canopy on the raft gave them some protection too. They were used to the sun and rain and it wouldn't take long to get used to the river.

Meta and Ugma had started keeping a daily log beginning with their last day at home. At first, there were many things to be done: wake up before the sun, quickly load the llamas, and then check each person to be sure they were ready to leave. Last of all, they made sure that nothing was left behind that would show the soldiers that they had been there. After a couple of days, they began to feel more relaxed and even looked forward to what the next hill or valley would bring.

Most of the villagers lived their entire lives within a few miles of the hut they were born in, so being introduced to these new sights was very exciting. As a wood carver, seeing the different trees kept Ugma interested. Were they hard or soft, light or heavy? Could they be carved or would he need an axe? Did they smell good was another thing to think about when choosing a particular tree to carve. Everybody liked good-smelling wood.

As each day passed, they thought less and less about the past and concentrated more on the present and what the future would bring. If Ugma heard anyone complaining, he would quickly point out that they were still alive and all of their neighbors were dead. "What can I do to help you?" Ugma would ask, and then he and Meta would do whatever they could to get them back on track. Usually they just needed a little reassurance that they were following their God's directions and it would be okay.

On the villagers went, day after day. The sailing had been so good that they kept going all night and all day. At first, the men took care of everything but, as time went on, they turned over more and more jobs to the women and children and, before long, they all shared the responsibilities equally. Arto was very pleased to see this take place. That had been his plan all along. Teach all the jobs to all the people and let them keep track of each other. It was a good idea, and it was working.

The river water was dark and murky looking from all the leaves floating in it, but it tasted good. They were still far enough away from the ocean so that it was not salty yet, as they had been warned it would be. So far, the only reason to go to the shore was to pick up food for the llamas and get fresh bananas for making inguiri, a mixture of cooked bananas and rice that they ate at almost every meal. By the end of the first week, they were at what is now the western border of Columbia and the river was running in a southeasterly direction. Ugma had already decided that they would stay with the river regardless of which way it went. The farther away from their village they went, the less they thought about the strangers and how close they had come to being killed.

Chapter 5

In many ways, the climate on the river wasn't any different from what they were used to—daily rains, high humidity, with the temperatures in the high nineties during the afternoon and dropping to the low eighties at night. Overall, they were quite comfortable and most of them were enjoying the trip.

The small problems that did come up had more to do with them being bored and not knowing what to do with their time. This was a new experience for them; they had always been so busy that there wasn't any time for boredom. Now with all this time on their hands, the memories of the things they left behind were gnawing on them and little squabbles were starting about who brought what and why.

It wasn't a big problem yet, but, left to itself, it could become one very quickly, so Ugma and Meta were trying to find things to keep everybody busy and not at each other's throats. Even the elders were having a hard time of it not knowing where they were going; there wasn't anything for them to plan for. Only the children were completely happy, living on a raft and fishing every day, just a few chores to do and enough responsibility for the operation of the raft to keep them interested and happy.

After nearly a month on the river, they came to a small village called Sao Paulo where Arto had the rafts go to the shore while he and two of the elders went into the village to purchase food and other goods they needed. No one else could get off the rafts and they had to be ready to leave at the first sign of trouble. Fortunately, there weren't any problems and soon Arto and the other elders came back with the supplies, ready to leave.

All the villagers wanted to go into the village to see what they could see, but Arto assured us that going into this village would not be a smart thing to do. As the rafts drifted away from the shore, small bands of warriors appeared in the clearings along the riverbank. Once again, Arto was right and, as they steered to the center of the river, they all sang praises to Arto and the Gods for keeping them safe once more.

After three more weeks on the rafts, they finally reached the junction of the Amazon River and Rio Negro. This was the most beautiful thing they had ever seen. It looked as though the entire world was covered with water. All you could see in any direction was water; the black water from the Rio Negro blending with the lighter colored Amazon River. If it hadn't been for the current of the river, they wouldn't have known where to go.

The three rafts rocked and churned at the point where the rivers joined, but the ones steering held them tight and soon they were drifting along again without any trouble. The speed of the current had slowed down a little and now they were traveling at a slower rate than they had been. With this change in speed, it became easier to steer the large rafts and, baring any other problems, they were all glad to be moving just a little slower.

Day after day, the only change that they noticed was that the river was getting so wide that they couldn't even see to the other side. It was so wide, in fact, they steered closer to the north shore where they were able to watch the forests and jungle along the way. Now that they were so well adjusted to their new way of life, the stops on shore got farther and farther apart. It was now necessary only to stop about twice a week, and then everyone was back on the raft ready to leave again in just a short time. The reason could be that they all wanted the trip to be over with and not wasting time on shore was a help.

Ugma was planning ahead to the day when the journey would be over and their new village was built. Then, once again, he could do the woodworking that he had trained so many years for and loved so much. The feel of wood to an artisan was like the touch of gold to a jeweler, and once that became a part of your life, there wasn't any way to get rid of it. Not that he would ever want to lose the feel for wood, but maybe when they reached their new home, there wouldn't be any need for a wood worker. If that ever happened Ugma told himself, he would retrain for a different kind of job, that's all there was to it.

Other people in this village have had to change their way of life, and so would he. However, in the meantime, he might just see if it was possible to make a better way to catch fish. There were so many different kinds of fish that you could not even name them all. Along the Orinoco, the river is one of the main habitats of the boto, also known as the Amazon River dolphin. The largest species of river dolphin, it can grow to lengths of up to 8.5 feet. Its most amazing characteristic is its color, which ranges, depending on its age, from soft, rosy pink to a vivid, almost shocking pink. The Portuguese name for this species in Brazil is boutu vermelho—red dolphin, color pink.

Surely, with all the people that eat fish every day someone had found an easier way to catch them. From today on until the end of the trip, Ugma would spend all of his spare time trying to find the answer. What needed to be found was a way for one person to catch several fish at one time without any help, and hopefully there wouldn't be any need for skill either. Probably, when the answer was found, they would locate someone who had already been doing it that way for a long time. Oh well, at least there was fishing to occupy his mind, for a while anyway.

It would seem good to use tools again Ugma thought. Actually, there hadn't been any reason not to have tools out and use them, but he just hadn't given it a thought. Today Ugma decided to make something nice for Meta. It had been a long time since he had a chance to do anything special for her, and for sure, she would appreciate it.

The trip was starting to show on her too. There are new lines around her eyes from worrying, so a gift would give her something else to think about. So far, all of her time had been spent trying to make everyone else more comfortable and doing any job that had to be done, not because it was her job, but because it was easier to do it than to find out who was supposed to do it, find them, and tell them they had a job to do. This was the kind of woman Meta was. She would pitch in, get the job done, and not worry about whose job it was; she would just do it and forget it. One reason their journey was running so smoothly, was people like her.

Late in the afternoon of the seventy-third day, Arto signaled that he wanted the rafts to turn in to the shore. This would be a welcome stop. Their last time on shore was five days ago and they were all getting a little restless. As they approached the riverbank, all eyes were looking for anything unusual in the trees or under brush. Arto had seen a large clearing on the bank, and he decided that they would be safer there than in a wooded section. They had traveled almost two thousand miles without trouble, and it would be nice if they could keep it that way for the rest of the trip.

The clearing was about five hundred feet along the riverbank and two hundred and fifty feet back in. That would give them plenty of room for protection, and they tied-up at the midway point. Only one third of the occupants from each raft were allowed on shore at a time, the rest stayed aboard ready for an emergency departure if it became necessary. So far, they had not needed to use the quick exit plan, but they were all ready just in case.

The shore group divided up with some of them going with Arto to the local village to purchase rice and bananas and other foodstuffs. The rest of them went with the two elders in search of feed for the llamas. It would be easy to just lie down and take a nap while they were tied up at shore, but Arto gave strict orders that everyone was to be alert and ready for a battle, if one should start. If everything went along quiet and without any problems that was fine too, but they had to be prepared, and that meant with weapon in hand, not on the floor or any place else. Arto spent a lot of time training them to defend themselves, and the first thing they had to do was *be ready*. They were ready.

When the group with the feed for the llamas came back, they got on the rafts and others went on shore to take a walk and exercise their legs. By the time Arto and his men returned, everyone had taken a turn on shore and helped load the provisions.

Soon the villagers were drifting out into the river to return to about a mile from shore. Now they could relax again. It's strange how quickly they all adapted to life aboard the rafts when three months ago none of them had ever seen a large raft. The answer had to be in the fact that they were the type of people that could be trained. They all had a trade, and no one was afraid of making changes.

Two important things happened as they drifted down the river. The first was that the river was so wide that several weeks ago they had to choose which side to be on and stay closest to that shore. The other change that they now noticed was that twice each day the level of the water in the river would slowly rise and then fall. When the water was low it was difficult to see the trees on the shore, but when it got higher, you could easily see the shoreline.

At first, they thought that there were hills and valleys in the river, but if that was the case, then why did it happen even when they were tied up at shore. There had to be an answer, of course, and one of these days, they would find it. For now though, they would just keep track of the changes and not worry about it.

There are many small islands in the river and when they had stopped at some of them, they found that they were not occupied. A small village on the riverbank was the ideal type for their needs, and then it was only necessary to make a short stop for supplies and leave again quickly. At the next place they stopped, Ugma would ask about the change in taste of the water, for some reason it tasted salty. Maybe it's a coincidence, but the only time the salt taste is in the water is when the river is deep, never when it's shallow. Surely, the local villagers will know why it is happening and if they have any reason to fear it.

When we found a place to stop, he told Arto what he had observed and asked if he could go with him into the village to find out what he could about the unusual changes in the water.

At first, the old man that he asked just laughed and said, "The ocean comes and goes two times each day and, when it does, it brings salt water with it. You are now very close to this big ocean, so you must carry your drinking water with you." When Arto heard that, he purchased eight large covered vessels for each raft to carry their drinking and cooking water.

Chapter 6

None of the villagers had any idea about plotting their course with the help of the stars and so, until the sun came up, they didn't have any way of knowing what direction they were traveling. There wasn't a thing they could do about it, but it would have been nice to know anyway.

When dawn arrived, it showed that they were moving in a northwesterly direction, almost the opposite that they had been going. Did that mean that they were being pushed right back into the shore? Only time would tell where they were going to touch land again. They had a six-week supply of food and water, so wherever they landed would be all right.

Throughout the day, the waves got higher and higher and it became difficult to see the other rafts. For some reason, the rafts traveled at different speeds, and they used the paddles to speed one raft up and slow the other ones down. This was the first hard work any of them had done in a long time and it felt good to use their muscles again. Tomorrow they wouldn't feel good but, for today, it was an opportunity to really loosen up. Ugma paddled so hard that he thought his raft would go from number three position up to the first place. This, of course, didn't happen. In fact, all his hard work may have even slowed them down a little.

There was no way for them to know that they were being pushed by the North Brazil Current, and that it would take them passed Guyane, and then Suriname, to Guyana. Even though they couldn't see land, they were actually not many miles from shore.

The weather continued to be hot and the wind and current pushed them farther and farther in a northwesterly direction. At times, they were close enough to the other rafts to shout to them and ask how they were doing. At other times, they drifted so far apart that they didn't see each other for many hours at a time. When this happened, they were all very concerned and the only thing that kept them from worrying was the knowledge that God was controlling their every move.

Every afternoon it rained. Sometimes very hard rain and the wind would blow and they would have to make sure that everything was tied down securely.

Without any reference points, it was difficult to tell if they were even moving. However, they had been traveling on the ocean now for more than three weeks and without knowing it, they had long since passed into the Guiana Current, which carried them in a westerly direction. Then, the Caribbean Current swept them between Cuba and the tip of Mexico where the Florida Current turned them more easterly, passed Cuba and around the Florida Keys.

Soon after, they entered the Gulf Stream and began following the coast of Florida. That first night, a storm struck so hard that they thought it would rip their cushmas right off their backs. The children and the llamas cried out in fear as the rafts seemed to jump out of the water one minute and go under the water the next. The worst problem though was keeping sight of each other. There wasn't a thing they could do except hold on and hope for the best. When the dawn finally arrived, the rain stopped and the waves settled back to a near normal level. The best surprise though was that all three rafts weren't any farther apart now than they had been before the storm.

The Gulf Stream was like a river in the middle of the ocean and they were lucky to be traveling in it. So far, the whole trip had been based on trusting the message that God had given them and being as prepared as they could be for each new situation.

As Ugma filled out his daily journal, the descriptions he gave would sound funny because most of the things he was writing about didn't even have names yet. The daily journal he was making would be used to teach the children and all the children after them about this long journey and why they had to make it. When they located the new village site, this journal would become the first permanent record and Ugma would carve a very fancy box to store the records in. This would be his personal contribution to all of their people.

They were moving north again and the storm had pushed them out of the Gulf Stream and toward shore. The weather was getting cooler now, and they all hoped that soon they would see land.

And they did!

Land on their left or west side could be seen in the distance, and Arto gave the signal for them to paddle to the shore as quickly as possible before another storm blew them away from land again. Paddling the rafts closer to the shore was a lot more difficult than they expected. The closer they got to the shore, they could see that there was a large waterway that divided the land, a river. They guided the rafts into the river straight ahead, and Arto chose to follow it for a while before going to the shore.

The water there was shallow enough, so they could use the poles again to push the rafts and, in a short time, Arto's raft reached the shore, and the other two waited until he had investigated the area and found it to be safe enough for them to land too.

This was a happy moment for everyone and Ugma said prayers of thanks to the Gods and announced that this was to be their new home. Not a person made a sound. Even the llamas were quiet. Could this really be their new home? Where were the hills and mountains? Where were the fast-flowing rivers and streams?

"Ugma, are you sure this is where we should build our new village?" Arto asked. Ugma assured him that in all his dreams since they left their homes, the same type of area stood out and this was it. They would be close to the ocean and their new skills of fishing and rafting could be utilized. In addition, almost everyone enjoyed swimming. When you took all of these things into consideration, the logical place for the new village was right there.

Chapter 7

Soon after landing, Arto and the other elders called for a meeting of the entire group. Arto explained that for the next day or two everybody would continue to live on the rafts and that the persons that would normally be steering would become the guards so that no one could sneak up on them. This seemed like a good idea and everyone readily agreed. The next day five men would search the area within three or four miles to see if there were any other villages nearby. Their instructions were to check first on the size and location of any camps or permanent settlements and then return and Arto would decide what they would do next.

Meta and Ugma walked a short distance into the jungle to see if they could find a good spot for their hut. Every place they looked was a good location; the problem would be in trying to find suitable building materials. In addition to that, Ugma didn't recognize any of the trees.

This sure was turning out to be a strange place when a wood worker couldn't identify any of the trees. We'll have to cut some down and find out what they are he thought. *Maybe I'd better wait until the search party gets back before I cut down any trees, because if this spot belongs to someone else, cutting down a tree might upset them. So, we won't do anything except look until they get back and Arto tells us what to do.*

Meta picked out a small clearing close to the river so that she wouldn't have to carry the drinking water very far. After that, she marked out a place for a garden and then for the hut itself. When the other villagers saw what the two of them were doing, they too began marking off the places for their huts and gardens. As soon as Arto became aware of what was going on, he ordered everyone to stop marking places for huts, and he would show them the village plan when the search group returned. Until they had checked to see if the area was claimed by anyone, they might just as well relax and take it easy. There was still a chance that they would have to find another spot.

Late in the afternoon, the men came back from their scouting assignment and told Arto that they had not seen any signs of people living there, or within four miles. Another meeting of the elders was ordered by Arto, and he said that his concern about settling here was because if this area was as good as they thought it was, then why were there no villages here or nearby. Something must be wrong with this place he reasoned, or it would be settled by now. They must find out first where the other villages were, and then they would pick a spot for their village. "Don't unload the rafts yet," he said. "We will continue to keep a guard on watch all night long for the present time. Tomorrow the scouting group will go farther out and away from us in search of villages."

Ugma asked Arto if he would call the entire group so that he could tell them about his latest dream. At first Arto declined saying, "We've already had too many meetings; besides, we have more important things to do."

Ugma asked Arto again saying, "My new dream affects everyone in this village, and I think they should hear it and decide for themselves."

Sig spoke up and said, "Why not tell it to all of us Arto? Ugma's dreams got us this far without any major problems."

Arto walked around kicking branches and shells out of his way then finally said, "Okay, Ugma, call the villagers and tell us your dream."

Sig and the other elders rounded up everyone and waited for Ugma to start.

Arto spoke first and said, "Ugma has heard from the Gods again and wants all of us to hear what they told him."

Ugma climbed up on one of the rafts so that they could all see and hear him. "Last night," Ugma said, "As I was trying to get to sleep, the Gods came to me and gave me new directions for all of us." Raising his voice a little he said, "When we got to the River Ucayali and divided our village into three different groups, one group to each raft, the Gods meant for us to stay that way from then on—three separate villages."

"Arto will head the new Village of Quint," he said, pausing for a moment. "Sig will head the second new Village of Montoro, and I will head the new Village of Chan."

No sooner had he said that then all of the villagers started yelling their approval.

Arto started to say something and then, while the group kept up their yelling, he decided that they had already voted so he might just as well keep quiet for now. But he vowed to himself that it wasn't over yet, no matter what the Gods told Ugma.

After the scouts had left, Ugma went looking for some wood to carve. There should be a lot of hard wood around and he was determined to find some. Even if it had another name, at this point all he wanted to do was to carve something because it was easier for him to think while he was working. Arto was right about this particular area not being settled. It seemed like such a perfect place to live, close to the ocean for fishing, a good supply of fresh water to drink from the river, and lots of trees. If we were not able to have mines for gold and silver here, then almost half of the people would need to learn another trade. Maybe it would be fishing, or at least something to do with the water. At any rate, none of them would starve to death.

When the scouts returned, they again reported that there weren't any villages in the immediate vicinity and the elders met to decide on whether or not they would stay there or move again. The meeting lasted several hours and finally Arto called the villagers together and told everyone that they would get back onto the rafts and sail north on the river until they reached a better location with nearby villages to trade with. Hopefully, it would be warmer too. Arto didn't know about the equator and the north and south poles or how traveling north now would take them to a colder area, not a warmer one. This he would learn as time went on. For now though, they would continue to go north until Arto was satisfied that they were indeed in the "promised land" that they had been searching for.

The three chiefs, with the help of the scouts, diligently plotted the way that they would travel up the Ak-lowahe (Ocklawaha) or Muddy River.

Several different ways were discussed, such as pulling the rafts, one at a time with long ropes that men on the shore could reach, while another group paddled as fast as they could. This was the plan that the chief's decided to try. A small group of children and the elderly would stay on the two rafts that were waiting, while the rest of them would pull and paddle the first raft through.

Hour after hour, the pulling and paddling continued and, at times, it seemed as though they hadn't moved an inch. To compound the problem of the swift current, the alligator population was so large that two men spent their time running up and down the riverbank yelling and driving them off with clubs. When darkness came, the entire group was ready to quit for the night.

The following day as they proceeded up the river, the current lessened and, by nightfall, the regular crew was able to paddle and pole the raft without any assistance from the men on shore.

Chapter 8

Arto, Ugma, and Sig decided that a small crew should be left on the raft, Chan, and the rest of them would walk back to the second and third rafts. At least five more days would be required to get all three rafts to this point, and then they would continue the trip towards their new home.

The work was very strenuous and, at the end of the day, everyone was ready for a good night's rest. Ugma and Meta talked and planned for their new village, and especially their own new home. Each night since the meeting when the group was split into three separate villages, Ugma said special prayers to the Gods and asked for guidance in selecting the proper location and the safest area for them to make their home. "I keep seeing the same place and how our village is laid out in my dreams, Meta. It's almost as though what I'm looking at has already been built." Meta tried to keep busy whenever Ugma talked about seeing things in his dreams, because she didn't really want to believe or disbelieve.

"If you really think you know how it's supposed to look," Meta said, "why don't you draw a picture and show it to me, and then I'll be able to recognize it too, when I see it."

Ugma picked up a stick, went to a cleared place in the sand, and drew an elongated "0." Next, he showed that the sun's path followed an elliptical route that traveled from right to left approximately through the center of the "0." The "0", he explained represented a lake, and the village was laid out on the right side in two rows, off-set like a "W", with a hut on each point and the doors facing away from each other, except for the center hut, and its doors faced down. This arrangement should give them maximum protection from attack.

"What I want to know is how close together the huts are going to be?" asked Meta. "Spreading them out too far will make it unsafe."

"I don't really know yet, but when I find the right spot, all I'll have to do is sort of squint my eyes and everything will be where it's supposed to be, just like in my dream."

Meta tried hard to believe in Ugma's dream if for no other reason than the fact that she was his wife and had faith in him, but maybe this was too much to ask of her.

Raft number two, Arto's Village of Quint, was the next one to be helped up the river. This took two days, the same as Ugma's did, and now they were almost through the difficult section of the river with Sig's raft, the Village of Montoro. By the time this day was over, all three of the rafts would be back together again. Tomorrow was going to be a day of rest and repacking on the rafts. The rough trip up the river had taken its toll in both men and equipment.

The alligators were so populous that everyone stayed on the rafts during the hours of darkness. All night long you could hear the "Humph-humph" sound of the alligators and every once in a while a thrashing in the underbrush. This thrashing probably meant they had caught their supper or at least they were trying to catch it. The three chiefs warned the villagers about how violent the alligators were and to avoid them whenever possible.

Three days later, they reached the inlet of Orange Creek and, although it was a nice spot, they continued up the Ocklawaha River. Mile after mile they poled the rafts following every twist and turn. The God's had indeed led them to a paradise.

From time to time, they would see signs that someone had lived here but they never did see a person. On and on up the Ocklawaha River the rafts were sailed and pushed or pulled. After several more days of traveling, they came to the junction of the Silver River. The water was so clear that it was impossible to tell how deep the river was. While the chiefs met to decide which direction to go, the rest of the villagers fished, and swam, and washed their clothes. The swimming didn't last very long though, because the water was so cold. Even the air was cold along the riverbank. This extreme change of temperature brought back memories of their mountain village in distant Peru.

After meeting for several hours, the chiefs decided to continue up the Ocklawaha River until a safe spot could be found to set up camp for a few days, while the scouts went on ahead. The water temperature returned to normal soon after they started up river again. Arto chose a spot where the river turned easterly, then south, then westerly again as the camping area and the rafts were soon secured to the trees on the bank. As soon as the area was checked for alligators and found to be safe, the llamas were unloaded and tied to trees on the creek bank where they could graze and also reach the water.

The other side of the river was all marshy swamp. After everything was secured and while most people were resting, Ugma took the smallest raft and paddled to the swampy area looking for an entrance. There were small waterway openings and he chose the first one wide enough to allow him to enter. After going just a few feet, it was impossible to see the river. He backed up to the point where he had entered the swamp and tied a large knot in a low hanging branch marking where he left the river.

This was a world that he had never seen before. Thick marsh grass and small trees were growing right out of the water. Islands divided the waterways and the underbrush was very thick. The stream he was following meandered around and every few feet he tied another marker knot. *After traveling as far as we just have, I sure don't want to get lost now.* Soon there was a larger island and he pulled the raft high enough on the shore to hold it while he looked around. Charred wood pieces, remnants of an old campfire, caught his attention. They appeared to be old because the rain had washed the soft char off and partially buried them in the sand. This was a good find. It proved that, whoever they were, they had visited this island.

The island was about one hundred feet in diameter and Ugma made a close check to see if anything was dropped or lost by whoever it was that built the fire. A few feet from the fire was a pile of fish heads and tails indicating that they had been there long enough to have several meals. Maybe the river goes up and down each day like it did on the Amazon and this island wasn't always above water.

Back on the raft again, he slowly passed the island and continued his adventure into the swamp. After checking six more small islands without finding anything, he turned around and followed his trail of knots back to the river and then to his own raft.

Arto was waiting for Ugma and Ugma told him what the swamp was like. Arto decided that it would be better if they just continued on the river and left the swamp alone.

While the sky in the east was beginning to show signs of the dawn, all three villages were busy reloading their rafts so that the journey to their new home could start again. The river was quite calm and easy to navigate but, because of the lack of wind, they had to paddle or pole the rafts.

On and on they traveled for five more days until they came to the outlet of Lake Griffin. The three rafts followed the eastern bank for a few more hours until it reached Haines Creek. As the rafts went up Haines Creek, Ugma stood on the front of his raft, Chan, and watched closely to see if any of the area looked familiar. He felt sure that he had seen this area before, maybe in his dreams. The bends and curves and even the trees on the banks of the creek were exactly as he had seen them many times in the past. "Meta, I know we are close to our new home. In fact, I can see the lake that I told you about." He got so excited that Meta asked him to have the rafts stop and tie up for the night.

Chapter 9

Arto ordered the scouts to prepare to check out the next two days run on Haines Creek to make sure that it would be safe and to report back as soon as they could. By this time, all of the villagers had congregated on the shore to watch as the scouts prepared to go up the creek.

"Sending the scouts won't be necessary," Ugma said. Arto looked to see who it was that dared to question his authority.

"You four scouts are to begin your journey now!" Arto shouted and he turned to face Ugma in an attempt to put more emphasis into his order. By this time, everyone from the three rafts were watching and listening to see what the outcome from this confrontation would be. The two men stood about fifty feet apart and just stared at each other. This isn't exactly what Ugma wanted to take place and, as he stood facing Arto, he wondered how it had happened.

"Was my voice too loud or gruff sounding or what was it that made it sound like a challenge?" Ugma whispered to Meta.

For a few seconds she just stood motionless and watched the reactions from the two men and the crowd. "Chief Arto, please allow me to speak." Arto squinted his eyes to see who it was that asked his permission to address the villagers and him. The mere fact that Meta had asked to speak had the effect of watering down the apparent challenge to his authority.

"Speak, woman," he shouted, and he folded his arms across his chest, stood very erect with his head back and his chin out, and waited for Meta to speak.

Meta walked about ten steps toward Arto and the villagers and then stopped and stood facing him. With outstretched arms, she addressed the crowd in her high clear voice. "My husband Ugma has no reason to challenge your authority Chief Arto when, in fact, he already has as much right to issue orders as either you or Chief Sig unless, of course, you don't plan to honor the vote of our people that divided us into three equal villages?"

Arto lowered his chin and turned his head ever so slightly in her direction before answering. "It is my duty and responsibility to send the scouts to check the route ahead of us," he shouted at her.

Meta shivered a little as she composed herself for this next round with Arto. "If you did not first consult with Chief Ugma and Chief Sig, then who gave you the authority to send the scouts out," she yelled right back at him. "Are we to believe that you consulted with the Gods themselves, and if you want us to believe that, then name the Gods that you spoke to."

Arto began to get fidgety because he knew that she was correct in thinking that he should have asked the other chiefs before sending out the scouts. All he could do now was to try to find a way to save face and not upset the villagers and every second he stood there without saying anything was making his chance of recovering the situation more and more difficult. "Woman, you are correct in what you say," he shouted, and a smile crossed his face as he added, "It is obvious that I have been wrong many times and apparently you are always right." As the chief turned away from her, the villagers began to laugh and cheer and Arto knew that the situation was now under control.

"Wait, wait everyone, I have more to say," Meta shouted. "My challenge to Arto about speaking to the Gods was a real one and not made in jest. Ugma has spoken to the Gods and they have revealed to him what lies ahead. You all know that Ugma has been with us at all times and also that no one has gone ahead up the river, yet he can draw a map of the river and the lakes that we are about to enter just as though he had been there. All of you come forward and look at the map that Ugma has prepared from the information that the Gods gave him."

With that, Ugma stepped forward and held the map he had drawn over his head so that they could all see it. "This is where we are now," he said pointing to a spot on the river. "This is a large lake that we will come to early tomorrow. There are many large and small lakes close by and with the help of the Gods, I have been able to see them all. Over here on this point of land is where the Gods told me to build the Village of Chan." The place he pointed to was the present city of Tavares, on Lake Eustis.

"This stream is called the Dora Canal to Lake Dora. The Dead River to the west ends at Lake Harris." Ugma continued to show the people where the Gods had told him to locate the three villages. Arto's Village of Quint should be on the west bank of the Dora Canal close to the lake. Sig's Village of Montoro should be on the west bank of the Dead River where it joined the lake.

Arto checked and rechecked the map to see if he could find any reason to doubt Ugma's story that the Gods had given him the information. *Well*, Arto thought, *they would all know tomorrow whether or not this was just a dream. If it wasn't just a dream, then he had better start making plans to capitalize on Ugma's ability or it wouldn't be very long before everyone would be going directly to Ugma and bypassing him.*

Arto suddenly remembered the four scouts and went to tell them to forget about the trip but, as he was walking, a plan began developing in his mind about how he could stay one jump ahead of Ugma and the help he was getting from the Gods. "Never mind about the scouting mission for tonight," he said. "It has been a long day for all of us. So, get some rest, and we'll get an early start tomorrow."

Chapter 10

As they walked back from the rafts, Arto signaled to his friend and head scout, Jon to hang back a little so that they could talk. The plan that evolved would have Jon study the map first and then, after the sun went down, he and one of the other scouts would sneak away from the group. If they were successful in getting out undetected, they would take a canoe and paddle up the river to the place where Ugma said they would find Lake Eustis. Assuming that they found a lake, Arto directed them to travel to the south-west corner and try to find the Dead River. From there they would travel easterly and try to locate the Dora Canal. When they finished checking the places marked on Ugma's map, they were to return to camp as fast as possible and quietly report their findings to Arto.

The most important thing to Arto was that regardless of what they found, he would know before anyone else and would use the information to his advantage. Even if Ugma was one hundred percent accurate with the map he drew, if Arto knew for sure that he was right, he could lead the villagers in praising Ugma and thereby retain his position as leader. Either way, Arto planned to retain the integrity of being the senior chief.

Jon studied the map and made mental notes about distances. In addition, he noted the locations of the canal and river with regard to their present position. As darkness fell, Jon searched for and found his partner, Luke, and they withdrew from the rest of the group and prepared to leave.

They quietly loaded the few things that they would need into the canoe and carried it upstream to a spot where they would not be detected. The canoe was lowered into the creek and Jon and Luke climbed in and paddled from shore. The night was still and the moon was just coming over the horizon as they paddled up Haines Creek to the lake.

The creek was wooded on both sides making it difficult to see when they actually entered the lake, but, sure enough, the lake was right where Ugma said it would be. After traveling east for about a mile, Jon changed directions and went due south. If Ugma's map was accurate, this would bring them right to the Dora Canal. The two men paddled for about forty-five minutes bringing them within a couple hundred feet of the canal, and on their left was a point of land jutting very prominently.

Jon tried to visualize the map again and as far as he could remember, it was perfectly accurate. Now, if they went west for a short distance, they should come to the Dead River. Following the tree-lined shore of the lake, Jon and his partner traveled first west then northwest for a couple hundred yards and then north. Just as Jon was ready to declare that Ugma's map was not accurate, he realized that they were parallel to and just a few feet from the entrance to the Dead River. They continued paddling and soon rounded the point of land separating the lake and river. It was just as he remembered it from Ugma's map. It was true then, the Gods really had spoken to Ugma.

The return trip didn't take very long, and soon they were at Haines Creek again looking for a place to hide the canoe. The entire trip took less than four hours and both men were tired, but Jon still had to report to Arto before he could go to sleep.

When Jon told Arto about the accuracy of Ugma's map, Arto was both surprised and pleased. Could it be that Ugma really was able to see into the future and, if so, Arto planned to exploit his ability to the fullest. This may turn out to be his lucky day. After thanking Jon, Arto promised to give him an extra share of gold when the division was made for being faithful to him.

Chapter 11

Arto laid awake the rest of the night formulating his plan. About an hour before the villagers awoke, Arto got up and began the preparations for his great plan.

Ugma and Meta had a restless night also. They were concerned about the way Arto was acting. Could it be that he didn't have any intention of relinquishing control of two-thirds of the present village to Ugma and Sig, not now, and maybe never? The transfer of power was supposed to come today, and Ugma sensed that Arto had other plans. One thing that he could be sure of was that Arto was a very smart man, and they would have to be alert at all times to keep ahead of him.

As the villagers awoke and started their daily tasks, the word was passed that Arto wanted a meeting of all fifty-nine of them as soon as possible.

"He sure isn't wasting any time," Meta told Ugma and Sig. "Half of them aren't even awake yet, and he's already moving in for the kill."

When they were all assembled, Arto stood on the bow of his raft looking down on them and waited until they were quiet. "My friends, I've called you together because I believe that now is the time to give thanks for the special powers that the Gods have bestowed on our brother, Ugma. These powers have guided us through the mountains of our homeland, the long journey on the Amazon River, the ocean voyage, and the rivers to where we are now. In addition to that, Brother Ugma is now able to see into the future and tell us how to lead our lives so we can be happy and prosperous. My friends, I beg of you to stand behind Brother Ugma and allow him to lead us in prayer, prayers of thanksgiving, and prayers for our future. Brother Ugma, will you lead us in this prayer?"

Arto reached a hand down to help Ugma up on the bow of his raft and, when he stood up, everyone cheered. Ugma tried to figure out just what it was that Arto was trying to accomplish with this big build-up. The important thing though, was that he knew Arto was up to something and he would be alert at all times. Ugma led them in several prayers and then jumped back down on the ground so that Arto could continue his speech.

"Thank you, thank you, Brother Ugma, for your fine prayers and words of promise and wisdom. We all thank you. We are fortunate my friends to have a person with the powers that Brother Ugma possesses. Yes ... yes, we are very fortunate, and that is why I called you all together, so that we might dwell just a few moments on these powers that he has. Is it fair for us to ask our Brother to accept the added responsibilities of being a chief when we can all see that his real calling is to be the spiritual leader for all of us? Is it fair I ask?"

So, that was the way he was planning to get rid of Ugma. Well, at least Ugma knew now what Arto had in mind, and Ugma knew that he would be expected to stand up right now and accept or reject Arto's plan. Accepting it would mean that the villages would stay the way they were, one large one with Arto as the chief. If, on the other hand, he rejected the plan, Arto would be able to quickly organize the villagers against Ugma for not being their spiritual leader and, in a sense, turning his back on the same Gods that just led them to this new land.

Ugma walked slowly to the raft again and accepted the helping hand from Arto as he climbed back up on the bow. The crowd was silent as he stood up and faced them. Ugma did not look down, instead, he looked up, up into the heavens and in a slow swooping movement he brought both hands out in front of him, with palms up and held them there as he addressed the Gods, and not the crowd that stood before him.

"My Gods, I thank you ... Yes ... I thank you, for you have given me more power than any other man that has ever walked in our midst. First, you allowed me to convey your message to our fine chief, Arto, that we would have to leave our homes and move to another land. Next, you guided me through the mountains and the rivers and oceans to this, our new homeland.

"Many months have passed since we first began this exciting new venture and, in this time, you have shown me how to lead and how to foresee the future. Yes ... I can clearly see the three new villages that begin today. First, is the Village of Quint with Arto as the chief. Second, is the Village of Montoro with Sig as the chief. Third, is the Village of Chan with me as not only the chief, but also the spiritual leader for the entire three villages. Again, I thank you, my Gods, for this special power that you have given to me."

Ugma looked down at the crowd then and said, "Chief Arto has served us well and deserves our thank you." Everyone cheered and cheered for Arto. "There is one more thing that I'd like to say," Ugma shouted as he motioned for them to be quiet and listen. "The Gods visited me in my sleep last night and told me that Chief Arto sent two scouts, Jon and Luke to see if my map is accurate. Tell us, Chief Arto, what did Jon and Luke find?"

Arto was in a state of near shock as he said, "Everything Ugma said is true, even the map is perfectly accurate." He then turned and walked to the back of the raft and began working on something.

Ugma called Arto back and said, "the Gods also told me that we should pick a spot here on the creek bank to bury most of our gold and silver until we need it." With that, Sig also climbed up on the raft with them.

"Why do the Gods think we should bury it here?" Sig asked, "since we are so close to our new villages."

"I don't know the answer to that question," Ugma said. "All I know is what the Gods told me, and I don't question them." Arto didn't look too happy either about digging a hole in the ground and packing the gold and silver in it.

"At what point do we stop following the instructions from the gods?" Ugma asked. "Do we just do what we are told when there isn't any other way?"

Both Arto and Sig squirmed over that comment. "I made a drawing of the place to dig the hole," Ugma said. "They were very specific in the location." He then unrolled the map that he had made and all three men looked at it. "Do you see these four trees?" he asked. "Well, there they are," and he pointed to a spot about fifty feet away.

The three men walked to the trees and then looked at the map again and there they drew a square on the ground about six feet by six feet just as Ugma had drawn. "Okay, men," Arto said, "let's start digging."

Because everyone was so anxious to get to their new villages, they decided to keep digging in shifts until the job was completed. While the men were digging, the women wrapped each bar of gold and silver in several layers of rough spun cloth and then placed them near the hole. Ugma took four men with him and they cut tree limbs to shore-up the walls of the hole to keep it from caving in on them as they dug.

When they reached the twelve-foot mark, they dug an antechamber off the main shaft. Soon they were sending down the limbs for the walls and floor. "Lower down the gold and silver," came the call from the shaft. One by one, the metal bars were lowered down the shaft and stacked in the side room. When that was complete, the three chiefs took turns going down and inspecting the room and its contents. Ugma was the last one to go down and, when he returned, he said, "Okay, men, lets fill it in."

A new crew started the reverse process and quickly the shaft was refilled and the excess was scattered in the woods. "Okay, everyone," Ugma yelled, "the reason we buried the gold and silver is that if we get robbed, we will still have most of it left, so each of you remember where it is."

"Are you all ready to go home?" Arto asked, and the final move was on again.

Chapter 12

Ugma's raft, Chan, pushed out into the creek turning upstream toward Lake Eustis; next came Arto in his raft, Quint; and last was Sig in Montoro. As they poled the rafts along, not a word could be heard. Total silence. All of them were deep in thought. Could they really be nearing the end of their long trip?

So many months had passed that it was hard to believe that soon they would be living in their own hut again, on solid ground! Meta made another mental list of just how her new hut would be. This was added to the lists she had made every day since they left home.

A cheer went up from everyone on the raft as it glided out into Lake Eustis and steered close to the shore on their right. Following the shoreline, they continued to the opening of the Dead River and stopped at the spot where the Village of Montoro would be built. Just minutes behind them, Arto too stayed close to the shore observing everything along the way. Pine trees and palm trees were everywhere. *This is good* thought Ugma. *All we need for our new huts is right here.*

Arto, on Quint, pulled up to the shore close beside them and he looked very pleased. "This spot is perfect, Ugma," Arto said. The two men jumped down from their rafts and waited for Sig and the Village of Montoro raft to arrive.

As Sig's raft hit the shore, he yelled to them, "I can see Arto's new village from here," as he pointed towards the opening to the Dora Canal.

The three men decided that all of them would stay here near the rafts while a group of scouts investigated the area around all three villages. As soon as the immediate area was cleared by the scouts, the llamas were unloaded. Ugma took a cup, filled it with water from the lake, and tasted it. "This is very good," he said, filling the cup again and handing it to Arto. Arto drank all of it and again filled it and gave the cup to Sig for his approval. Soon the entire group was testing the water and then they tied the llamas so that they could drink too.

Some of the boys got out their fishing lines and fished off the back of the rafts. Within minutes, one of them yelled, "I got one, a big one!" And sure enough he did.

This fish was different from any they had ever seen and the boys brought it to the three chief's to inspect. "Look at the size of its mouth," said Sig. "It goes back beyond its eyes." The men looked it all over and decided that it would be good to eat so the boys could keep it.

"Since we don't know what kind of fish it is," said Ugma, "let's just call it Big Mouth."

Every couple of minutes another boy would yell, "I got one, a big one!"

This continued until they had about fifty fish in the pile. "Okay, boys," Sig said, "it's time to stop fishing and start cleaning the ones you have. You have enough for a big meal for all of us now." The dozen boys worked fast cleaning the fish and soon the job was complete. After the fish had been equally divided between the three rafts they buried the leftovers and went back to the lake for a swim.

Before long, the scouts were back reporting that the area around this side of the Dead River was safe for them to use. Arto told all of the villagers that they were free to roam around and check out whatever they wanted to, but if they kept the water in sight, they wouldn't get lost. Soon, fifty plus men, women, and children were scampering in all directions admiring this wonderful location that the Gods picked out for one of their new homes.

Sig took charge of the adults from his village of Montoro and they started the task of setting a spot for each new hut. Early on, they made plans to use the "W" formation that the Gods told Ugma to use so all they needed to do now was to decide how big the "W" would be and assign a hut to each place. Each family group picked out their own location and Sig gave his approval. That turned out to be the easiest thing that they had encountered on the whole trip, and everyone was happy.

After the hut locations were completed, Sig told them his plan for construction. "Every hut will be built pretty much the same as in our old village," he said. "The exception will be any small changes a family wants to make their hut better for them. First, we need to decide on the overall size of each hut and then make a list of the material for that hut. We all need to continue to live on our raft until all of the huts are complete.

"I would like each family to mark out the size of their hut," Sig said, "just take a stick and draw it on the ground." With that, each family group went to their location and started the process of drawing out the dimensions of their new home. That's when the squabbling began. The men wanted a big hut with plenty of space and the women wanted a smaller one. It was the same with almost all of the families. Even Sig's wife objected to how big he wanted their new home.

Just before suppertime, the scouts came back and announced that all of the villages were safe to move to. With that good news, Ugma called his village together and told them to get everything back on the raft because "We're going home!"

Arto called his village and they loaded up too, ready for the final move. As the rafts moved away from the shore, they yelled their goodbyes and then Ugma led the way to the western edge of the Dora Canal where the Village of Quint would be built. Arto, Ugma, and the other men walked around where the huts would be built discussing the pros and cons of using the "W" layout like the other village. After several minutes of back and forth banter, Arto marked out the big "W" on the ground and told the men to pick the location for their home and mark it.

After the individual home spots were marked, the women and children got off the raft and came to join them. They all seemed very happy with the choices.

This only took a few minutes, and then the rest of them were off again to their own new Village of Chan. The lake was peaceful and calm and their raft moved easily along the shoreline until Ugma yelled, "We're home. Pull in right there by that big tree." When the raft hit land, three men jumped off and secured it to the tree. Then Ugma asked everyone to get off the raft, form a circle, and together they thanked the Gods for their new village.

"Since we have so much room, I'm going to make our 'W' stand on its end instead of the way the other villages are," Ugma said. Taking several long pieces of cloth, he proceeded to tie them to trees marking out the new village. Each leg of the "W" was about three hundred feet long so that the individual huts would have plenty of space between them.

Ugma and Meta's hut was on the tip of the center of the "W" (at the present-day junction of Orange Avenue and Nelson Street in the City of Tavares) with the door facing the lake and also looking over all of the other huts. There were five huts in all for the nineteen of them with plenty of room for expansion as their families grew.

While the men marked out the village, the women moved the cooking unit off the raft into a nearby clearing and started cooking fish and bread for the first meal in their new village. Soon the smell of the cooking fish filled the air and everyone gathered for supper. They were so excited that they walked around carrying their food with them looking here and there pointing out new things to each other in a child-like fashion.

Ugma and Meta sat on the ground on the spot where their new home would soon stand lazily daydreaming about what the future would hold for them. None of them had ever been responsible for providing food for their family because they had hired men in a nearby village to hunt for them. Number one on the learning list would have to be hunting. *Over time, the bows and arrows we now have will wear out and maybe that's what my new profession will be*, Ugma thought, *designing and constructing the hunting equipment.*

Ugma too decided, as the other villages had, that they would all continue to live on the raft until all of the new homes were built. When the construction job was complete, they would all move on the same day. If nothing else, it would keep the arguments to a minimum about whose house was first.

It was getting dark now as Ugma and Meta strolled back to the raft taking their time to stop at the spot where their neighbor's homes were going to be built and chatted with all of them. "This is such a wonderful location for our new village," Meta said. "Tonight we should send special prayers to our Gods for sending us here."

Chapter 13

Construction of the huts went along quickly taking about a week for each one and soon moving day was upon them. What a happy day that was! A few minutes before the sun came up, they all assembled in front of the raft. Their Village of Chan consisted of Ugma and Meta in hut number one. Hut number two had a young couple with one daughter and her grandmother. In hut number three was a couple with his father plus their two children, a teenaged girl and a boy. Number four consisted of a couple and three teenagers, a girl and two boys. The fifth hut had a couple and a seven-year-old daughter.

"Let's go home," Ugma yelled and the big move began in earnest. By the time the sun came up over the lake, each of the five huts was bustling with activity. Each evening during the construction period, the men worked building their own furniture, which consisted of a table for both the inside and the outside and the fire stand several feet in front of the hut. The women wove palm fronds into mattresses that hung on the walls during the daytime. In addition, they made special things for their home.

Ugma helped each family with their special projects while the hut construction was in progress so that they might all have something new for their home. Before he became a chief, he hadn't spent much time being concerned about anyone except the two of them unless he was asked. It was different now; it was his job to ensure the safety and happiness of the people in his village. During the past few weeks, they had enjoyed fresh fish for most of their meals but now they all wanted to eat some of the deer and rabbits that frequented the area.

The bows and arrows they brought with them appeared too crude and one of Ugma's first projects was to make improvements on both. Starting with a fresh piece of cedar limb, he first stripped the bark off then, with his knife, he scraped and smoothed the bow with a taper running from a three-inch center area to each end. The overall length was about forty-two inches. On the ends, he carved a notch for the string.

Using a piece of cured rawhide, he cut and fashioned the string, testing and tightening as he carefully bent the bow into shape. This was the critical part of his new bow; a more slender and graceful appearance which also meant it would be stronger and lighter in weight. Cutting the bark from the limb into small pieces, Ugma boiled them in water to make the dye for darkening the wood. This was a trick he learned as a wood carver. The longer the bark boiled, the darker it got and, after a couple of hours, it was just right. Ugma used a piece of cloth tied to a short stick for the dyeing process being careful not to spill any on himself.

After allowing the bow to dry for a while, he used a piece of soft leather to rub the dye into the wood. It took six different dyeing steps to make the bow as dark as he wanted it. Then came his special touch as he carved a small llama, deer, and dog on the bow as he had on the boxes in the past. When the bow was finished, he tightened the string until it was very taught, bending the ends over several inches giving it a whole new appearance. He then fashioned the handgrip area and applied a thin piece of leather tying it tightly on both ends.

Placing an arrow on the bow, he pulled the string back until he couldn't pull any more. Taking careful aim at a tree about fifty feet away, he let it go … swish and the arrow took off, straight as a string burying its head into the tree. "Wow!" Ugma yelled, "We'll have lots of fresh meat now." Hearing Ugma's yell, the villagers quickly came and gathered around him to see what the noise was about. When the men and older boys saw Ugma's new bow, they all wanted to try it out. Each, in turn, sent an arrow zipping through the air to its intended target. The response was unanimous; they loved it and wanted Ugma to make them each a new bow.

Ugma explained that each bow took several hours to construct and he would make them in exchange for their labor doing jobs he would have been doing if he wasn't making bows. They all readily agreed to the arrangement and soon each one that wanted a new bow was scurrying the woods looking for the perfect limb. When all of the limbs had been gathered, Ugma had them put their own mark on the limb to keep them straight.

Shortly after noon, two of the men and the three teenaged boys decided to go on a hunting trip. One of the men borrowed Ugma's new bow and off they went in search of some fresh meat for supper. Ugma told them to take some marking threads and mark their trail because the area was still very new to them. It wouldn't take long before they would all know it by heart and even the little ones would be free to roam.

Walking easterly, they soon found a small lake on their left and another one on the right and straight ahead was another small lake. They walked another mile or so and directly in front of them was Lake Saunders. While they stood admiring the lake, one of the men put his finger to his lips to quiet them and shortly a large buck deer walked out of the woods and started drinking from the lake.

Selecting a long slender arrow from his pack, the man with Ugma's new bow crept slowly closer to the buck deer. When the deer finished drinking, he raised his head and turned slightly placing himself broad side to the hunter. Zip! And away the arrow went through the air finding its mark slightly behind the right shoulder. "Ug-ha," snorted the big buck as it staggered trying to keep its balance. Then, slowly, the deer eased down and lay on the ground dying. The five hunters ran to the deer admiring the large rack of horns. It had one, two, three, four, five, six, seven, eight tips! Eight short tips on a very large set of horns! What a happy day this was. They yelled and praised each other on being such great hunters.

Now came the task of moving the deer to their village. Fashioning two long sticks with the backpack from one of the men tied as its center, it formed a crude "H" and the deer was placed on it. The three teens and one of the men each took a pole end and away they went toward home, five very happy young men, and one very large deer.

As the hunters got closer to their Village of Chan, they started yelling for everyone to come and look at their prize. All of the men, women, and children gathered around the deer admiring how large it was. Their main meat up until now had been sheep and goats and the sheer size of this fine animal almost overwhelmed them. The women quickly gathered their utensils and began the task of cutting and dividing the meat. A large chunk was given to each family to cook now and the rest was cut into thin strips and hung up to dry. Next they scraped the inside of the skin as clean as they could, rubbed it with salt, and stretched it on some limbs that were tied together just for that purpose. Two of the men then hung the skin in a tree to dry and cure.

Just before the sun set, Ugma called the villagers together and they joined him as he said a prayer of thanksgiving to the Gods. "Oh God of sun and water and food," he prayed, "thank you for blessing us with this beautiful new land to live in and our new homes and good water to drink and fish and deer to eat." He paused briefly and then said, "You carried us out of our homeland always keeping us safe from the soldiers and to the great river where you built large rafts for our journey. Week after week we floated down the river and then into a great ocean where we continued to float for more weeks and finally into another river and then here to our new home." Ugma paused a few moments and then asked, "Who else would like to thank our God?"

One by one, the men took their turn thanking and praising God for their good fortune and asking for a special blessing for their family and home. When they were finished, they all went home to enjoy the deer meat that had been cooking all afternoon.

For the next several days, Ugma worked on the bows and arrows for the other men in his village. As each was completed, he would present it to the new owner and watch as they used it the first time to be certain that they were satisfied.

Chapter 14

Several weeks after their arrival, Ugma began a new project constructing a small box about six inches by six inches by twelve inches long for Meta to hold her personal things. Because of its intended use, the box was made like two triangles that slid together instead of being a rectangle with a top and bottom. Hour after hour, he carved until the top and bottom slid together perfectly and securely. Then began the most important part, carving the inside of the box with special things that Meta would want: a llama, a dog, trees, and an assortment of flowers. In the top, he carved a map to the location where the bulk of their gold and silver was stored. After completing the inside of the box, he carefully reassembled it and then carved the outside with scenes from their village in Peru.

Next, he mixed some colors to stain the different animals and flowers and give it the appearance of a small painting on wood. The project had taken him several weeks, part-time, to complete and was it beautiful! As Ugma sat holding the box and admiring it, he was struck by a flash of genius. Put a set of hinges on it and make it look like a regular box. Wow! That would be fun, watching Meta try to open the box in the regular way and not being able to open it. It would keep other people from getting it open too.

Now that the box was complete, he decided to make something special for Meta to put into it as a remembrance of their long voyage. Ugma's share of the gold and silver consisted of three bars of gold and seven bars of silver, each approximately two inches by four inches and twelve inches long. The balance of the gold and silver was left in the storage pit for future use.

He began by sketching different animals: a llama, then a dog, then a dog with a llama. Next, he sketched a cat, and a cat with a dog. Trees were always nice too. What he really needed was something about their trip. "The raft!" he said to no one in particular, "a golden raft."

Ugma spent the next few nights sketching different views of their raft, Chan. Then the real work began. Carefully he shaped gold from one of the gold bars into thin strands about two feet long. Laying the strands of gold out, he shaped them into the outline of the raft. Next, he took smaller strands and fastened them together holding the shape of the raft. This took several hours a day over the next week.

Once Ugma was satisfied with the shape, he began the tedious job of filling in the center area. Using one or two strands of gold at a time, he tried to imitate the actual construction of the raft using gold instead of the straw and balsa wood used on the original raft.

Next, he placed several people on the raft including an over-sized version of himself. With three people on each side of the raft rowing, it was complete.

Ugma wrapped the gold raft in several layers of fine cloth, then gently guided it into the box, and then slid the cover into place. Now it was time to put it back in the hiding place until it was time to present it Meta.

Life in their new village was good for all of them to the point that they talked less and less about their former home and even the trip that got them there. Late in the week, the wind began to get stronger and stronger and the clouds appeared to fly across the sky. All night long, the wind blew higher until, when morning arrived, they all got busy and picked up and secured whatever they didn't want to get blown away.

Several men helped to pull the raft, Chan, up onto the shore so that the wind wouldn't tear it apart. Ugma called everyone together to plan how they would protect themselves during the night time, especially if the wind got any stronger. They all agreed that each family should stay in their hut unless and until it too blew away. At that point, they fully expected the wind to die down during the night.

But it didn't. The wind got stronger. Shortly before midnight, a really strong gust of wind ripped the entire roof off Ugma's hut taking most of the contents with it. He and Meta lay on the floor holding on to each other and the posts that supported the roof. With each new gust of wind, they heard other villagers scream as their hut was blown away but there wasn't any way for them to help.

Hour after hour, the wind grew stronger until first Meta and then Ugma was blown away too. Everyone in the three villages perished in the giant hurricane. Nothing was left to show that they had even existed except the cleared space where their huts had stood. The wind had probably reached two hundred miles an hour. It was a real "killer" hurricane.

The box that Ugma had built for Meta and placed the golden raft into was blown into a cypress tree and wedged into the roots.

Epilogue

The pool was complete, our lives were taking on a more leisurely pace, and once again we were able to think about the box. Although we hadn't spoken much about it for several weeks, we both knew that we had some burning questions that needed to be answered.

After the girls retired to their bedrooms to do homework and get ready for bed, Gail and I went to my shop, placed the box on the work bench, and pondered the situation—a box with no obvious top or bottom but with a shiny set of hinges. "Okay, Gail," I said. "it's time to get out the big hammer and give it a few sharp taps to loosen it up. Maybe there's a seam, but it's packed with dirt, so that we can't see it."

Gail held the box while I tapped it, first on the ends, and then on the top. Nothing moved. No dirt was dislodged either exposing a seam. After a couple of hours, we decided to put the box away for the night and tackle it again in the morning.

The girls left for school at 7:45 a.m. and soon after Gail and I, with fresh cups of coffee in hand, headed for the shop. As we were passing through the living room, Gail said, "Let's sit a minute while I tell you about the dream I had last night."

"I didn't hear you laughing or screaming, so it couldn't have been funny or scary," I said. "So, what was it?"

Gail kicked off her shoes and sat on the couch with her feet up under her, and I said, "Wow, this must have been quite a dream, and long too the way you got yourself so comfortable for the telling."

She started by saying, "We both have been concentrating on the obvious ways a box is constructed so that we may have missed the not-so-obvious ways. In my dream, I saw the box being opened from end to end, top corner to bottom corner." She placed her hands apart with one higher than the other hand. "I think the hinges are for decoration, but the box opens from corner to corner, like this," and she moved her hands closer together with the left hand higher than the right hand.

"Gail honey, I think you've got it," I said, "but before we try it, what was the rest of your dream?"

"I believe that the box contains something very valuable, not worth thousands of dollars, but millions of dollars," she said.

I put my arm around Gail and told her," I believe in your dreams, and now let's see if we can make them come true."

We walked together to my workshop and placed the box on the bench. Gail tipped the box so that the hinges were in the upright position. Then she placed one hand on each end of the box, left hand high and right hand low and pushed. Nothing moved. Then she switched hand positions and tried again. This time I reached around her and pushed with her and, lo and behold, the two ends started moving.

We both kept pushing until the two pieces slid apart. "Gail, I don't believe it!" I said. "The box is open!" The first thing we saw was how beautiful the designs were on the inside walls of the box.

"They look similar to the outside pictures," Gail said, "but the color is very clean." "That guy in Orlando would go nuts if he saw this," I said.

Packed in the box was something wrapped in a burlap type of material. It filled the entire box. Carefully I picked up the cloth-like covered object and placed it on the bench. "You do the honors and unwrap it, Gail," I said. "It was your dream that got the box open."

Carefully, Gail unwrapped the cloth, turn after turn until it fell off exposing a gold-colored raft with several miniature people on it.

"Holy smokes," I said. "That is the most beautiful thing I've ever seen. It looks like pure gold."

I looked at Gail and the tears were running down both cheeks of her face. "Here," she said, "you hold it. It must weigh five pounds, and it's so delicate."

Gently, I picked up the golden raft from her hands, careful not to bend or twist anything and was amazed at how heavy it was. Under the bench, I stored a postal scale, so I reached down, picked it up, and placed it on the bench. Then I put the golden raft on the scale, and it read just a fraction over ten ounces. "Well, it may not be five pounds," I said, "but it's still pretty heavy."

Gail picked up the gold raft and turned it from side to side and over and back looking for something.

"It doesn't say 'Made in China' on it anywhere, does it?" I laughed.

"No," she said. "It doesn't say 'made in anyplace'."

"Then it must be an antique," I said, "and you know how I love antiques." I put our digital camera on the short tripod and, with the gold raft sitting on the postal scales, I took several pictures. The first with the raft turned sideways and the scale facing forward so that the ten-plus ounces showed in the picture.

Next, I took several pictures of the inside of the box. The paintings looked like a slide show, similar to the outside of the box, but in full color. On the inside-top there was a carving that looked like a map of some type. It showed a large lake and then a small river or stream off one side and a large river and then a smaller one on the end and partly up one side. On the side of the smaller stream, there was a "circle" with a small mark inside. "You know, Gail," I said, "the box may be as valuable as the gold raft, so we really have two antiques, not just one."

"It looks like we have company," Gail said. "A white pick-up is parked in our driveway."

"Darn," I said. "We better put our toys away. It might be our friend from Orlando."

Soon there was a knock at our back door and, when we got there, it was the salesman from the pool company. Opening the door, I said, "Good morning. What brings you out so early in the morning? Do you want to take a swim in our new pool?"

"No," he said. "I just stopped by to make sure you folks were happy with your new pool and that we met your expectations."

"Well," I said, "on a scale of one to ten, you people rate a fifteen! Everything is better than we expected." Taking out his pen and notebook, he said, "Can I quote you on that?"

"You sure can. We just love it."

"I didn't want to tell you before," he said, "but you are my first customers, and I'd like to take you two out for lunch."

"Well, that sounds just great. Where shall we go, Gail, McDonald's, or Wendy's? or did you have somewhere else in mind," I said. Since he wasn't familiar with our area, he left the choosing up to us.

"As long as we're going out to eat," Gail said, "I'd like some pancakes at I.H.O.P. Is that alright with you two?" And away we went to I.H.O.P.

After a leisurely breakfast and a few cups of coffee, we returned home and said our goodbyes. "That was a great idea," I said. "We should do that more often."

"Gail looked at me and said, "If we eat like that every day, we'll both weigh four hundred pounds. Let's try once a week.

The following day, after our morning chores, I went into my shop and retrieved the box from its hiding place. First, we laid out prints that had been made from the designs on both the inside and the outside of the box in what appeared to be the correct order. Gail taped the pieces together making one long continuous sheet for each.

Next, she laid out the many pictures we had taken, and we sat there looking at what we had:

1. The golden raft
2. The decorated wooden box

3. The prints we had made from the box, both inside and outside

4. The pictures

We both just sat there and looked at our collection.

"Suppose," I said, "We take a ride to Gainesville to the University of Florida and check their museum for another golden raft? This time we won't make the mistake of talking to anyone about what we have; we'll just look at what they have and ask questions."

Gail checked the computer for information on the University of Florida at Gainesville, while I looked for any information I could find about golden rafts on Google.

"Gail, take a look at this," I yelled. "This is what we've been looking for, and we won't have to go to the university after all."

==========

Cultura Muisca

From the time leading Spanish Explorer Cortez, while in Mexico, saw large emeralds and heard about the wealth coming from tribes far to the south, the Spanish empire set out to find the riches and treasures hidden somewhere in the jungles and mountains to the south.

In 1537 the Spanish explorers ventured deep into what is now Colombia heading straight south from the Caribbean through the waterways and the great river called the Magdalena. Facing repeated attacks from warrior tribes like the Taironas at the mouth of the river and others farther up river, the Spanish felt unsettled about their new route to wealth and riches in this new land. They had even considered this river a potential route to Peru.

Spanish explorer, Gonzalo Jimenez de Quesada's troops, journeyed far up river and began to meet up with peoples native to the area. These "Muiscas" were different from previously encountered tribes. They were far more peaceful and seemingly even more "civilized". The Spanish explorers mention in their diaries that these natives dressed in better clothing and their living structures, though made of straw and mud still, were constructed with superior engineering to that of the lowland tribes farther north.

The Muisca culture was based on two supreme rulers called the Zipa and farther south called the called the Zaque. These were considered as almost god like beings by their subjects and were never to be looked at directly.

The Muiscas anthropologically are a subculture of the larger Chibcha tribe. The Chibchas were the biggest people group between the Aztecs of Mexico to the north and the Incas of Peru to the south.

The Muiscas used sacred lagoons and forests for sacrifices and the burial of offerings of emeralds and gold artifacts. The natives would bury the offerings as only the Caciques or chieftains were allowed to throw the artifacts directly to the Gods in the bottom of the sacred lagoons.

One lagoon in particular spawned the famous legend of El Dorado, the "Golden One". Farther up in the mountains than any

of the villages, about 3000 meters above sea level, lies the small round crater lake or lagoon of Guatavita. The deep round crater was thought to have been created by a meteorite strike about 2000 years ago. The Muiscas believed it was the coming of the Sun God who from then on inhabited the bottom of the lake.

The most intriguing stories that drew the Spanish Conquistadors from Peru northwards and southward from Mexico came from stories of the ceremonies surrounding the crowning of the great Caciques. When the Zipa died, his body would be entombed in a gold casket and thrown into the sacred lagoons. The new Zipa would be specially crowned in this particular hidden deep-cratered lagoon called Guatavita. He would be covered in honey or other sticky substances and then gold dust, thus visually seen to be "El Dorado". He would then be sent out into the middle of the lake on a small reed raft with some of his most important subjects. The raft would have many golden artifacts and emeralds strewn about his feet. In the middle of the lake, the artifacts were thrown overboard and the new Zipa would jump in washing off the gold covering his body.

A historical description of the ceremony was written up about 100 years after the first explorations:

"... By that lake of Guatavita they made a great raft of reeds, decorating it as beautifully as they could ... They undressed the heir, anointed him with a sticky earth and dusted him with ground and powdered gold, so that he went in the raft completely covered with this metal. The golden Indian made his offering, casting all the gold and emeralds he had brought into the middle of the lake, and the four chiefs who were with him made their own offerings; and when the raft landed the feast commenced, flutes and horns, with great dances in circles according to their custom, with which ceremony they received the new ruler and acclaimed him their lord and prince. From this ceremony came the celebrated name of El Dorado." Juan Rodríguez Freyle, 1636 (from Museo del Oro: Bogota Colombia).

The search for treasure then began to focus on this lake, but with very few rewards. Many items were found but the depth and difficulty of diving and exploring these waters in this crater proved the Crater Lake to hold its mystery.

In 1578, the Spanish merchant Antonio de Sepulveda secured a license from Spain to drain the lake to gain access to the incalculable treasures lying beneath the waters. With large numbers of Muiscas, he ordered a slice of the side of the crater to be dug away to drain the lake. This missing chunk can be seen today, and although it took the water level down some, the lake only surrendered 10 ounces of gold.

Many years later in 1801, Alexander van Humboldt initiated an enterprise to widen this gap in the side of the crater. The water level was lowered but only a few pieces of gold were discovered. In 1912 the English company Contractors Ltd. was able to drain more of the lake finding many pieces of gold, but it still did not cover the £40,000 investment.

The legend still keeps attracting treasure hunters to try and explore the lake and find its largest treasures still hidden in the dark cold and murky waters.

The little golden raft named the "Balsa Muisca" now on display at the Gold Museum in Bogota is the most representative symbol of this whole story. Some claim it was found in the lake during one of the treasure hunting expeditions. Probably the most accurate version comes from the Gold Museum historians who document that 3 farmers found it hidden inside a ceremonial Muisca clay pottery jar far south of Bogota in a cave close to the little town of Pasca back in 1969.

The raft itself was cast in the Muisca "Tumbaga" method of lost wax in clay mold. The Museum says that it was cast in a single piece out of 80% gold and alloy with copper and native silver. It weighs 287.5 grams and measures 19 cm long x 10.1 cm wide x 10.2 cm high.

==========

Peering over my shoulder, Gail read the story about the golden raft on the computer screen. "Well," she said, "it looks like those folks are in for a surprise when they find out there are actually two golden rafts and one of them will be for sale to the highest bidder."

"Whoa," I said. "What do you mean, to the highest bidder? Don't you remember what that man in Orlando said about everything belonging to the State of Florida?"

"Yes, I remember, but I also read in the newspaper about how our wonderful state ties everything up for years, and then they may pay only ten percent of the actual value." The word "may" is what bothers me. Why, we could be dead and buried by the time the state gets around to paying us.

"Let's find out what the value of the other golden raft is and then we'll make our decision," I said. "In fact, I'll start looking right now."

After finding the website for the *Museo del Oro: Bogota Colombia,* I checked to see if they had an English version, which they did, as they had thousands of English-speaking visitors each year. Pretty soon, they will be able to add the four of us to their rolls. The sad part is that our daughters won't know why we're going to Columbia, except for a different kind of vacation. They'll probably love it.

I kept searching to find the name of someone of authority but without any luck. "According to their website, they have more than 20,000 gold pieces and the golden raft is more valuable than all of them put together," I said. "Since we know what they have, and we know what we have, I think it's time to look for someone that buys South American antiquities. Those gold coins could be worth as much as $50,000,000."

"While you're looking," Gail said, "look for information on a Swiss numbered bank account. We'll probably need one."

"Darn, that was fast," I said, "from a swimming pool in the back yard to a Swiss bank account without passing 'Go'."

Finding how to open a Swiss numbered account was easy enough, all we needed was some money. "Some of the banks require as much as $500,000.00 to open an account," I said.

"That's the kind I want," Gail laughed. "And, while you're at it, let's get a minimum withdraw of $100,000.00. We can't be picky about spending some—"

"Hey, look at this," I said. "There's a special at Delta Airlines with four round-trip tickets to Bogota and a week at a four-star hotel for just $870.00 each."

"And just how do you propose getting our golden raft out of the country?" Gail asked.

"I guess I'll just have to think about that for a while," I answered.

The End

Watch for book two,

The Golden Raft Comes Home.

About the Author

Meet Dennis Michael Dutton who, in his eightieth year, decided to write a book. He had been working on Stepson for twenty years and, after purchasing a Kindle Fire HD said, "Heck, I can do that." And he did.

But he didn't stop there. He wrote *Stepson, The Golden Raft, The Golden Raft Comes Home, After the Golden Raft, What the Heck Have You Done Now, Kate?*, and *The Rose of Majorca*.

These books are available as electronic books or as paperbacks.

If you like them, please leave a review. If you love them, then leave a better review.

CPSIA information can be obtained
at www.ICGtesting.com
Printed in the USA
BVHW041305281220
596574BV00019B/243